JN071049

SMALL WORLD

Maya Inoue

Translated by Keiko Yonaha

スモールワールド

井上摩耶　英日詩集

訳　与那覇恵子

Coal Sack Publishing Company
Tokyo, Japan

コールサック社

SMALL WORLD
スモールワールド

A Collection of Poems in English and Japanese

英日詩集

Maya Inoue
井上摩耶

Translated by Keiko Yonaha

訳　与那覇恵子

Coal Sack Publishing Company
Tokyo, Japan
コールサック社

CONTENTS

I
Passing Shower

Passing Shower

Standing under the roof
during a passing shower in early summer
I smell the dust
thrown up by the rain.

Greens may be happy now.
Flowers and plants,
rice fields and vegetable fields—
all may be happy now.

People are busy looking for roofs and umbrellas.
But rain is necessary for Nature.
It is strange
that we are living together.

The cherries are out of bloom.
Ginkgoes come into buds.
Like a graduation,
they change like a human heart.

If there is a land in my mind,
what smell does it have?
Is it this smell of dust?
Is it this smell full of tenderness and strength?

The asphalt road is wet.
Cats fall into a doze.
Opening the window,
I'm enjoying the smell.

Far away
a pigeon coos.

A Lady Painting a Sandhill

When did she start?
I don't know.
She is a lady
painting a sandhill.

Charmed by a sandhill,
visiting various sandhills,
bringing back the sand,
she mixes it into the paint and begins.
She keeps on painting as if it would last forever.

Why is she so charmed by a sandhill?
She said,
because it changes every moment
never the same.
The beautiful ripples will soon disappear.

I love the lady.
For a long time,
for many hours,
she simply continues to paint.
She is tough and dignified.

Now my heart is dry like a sandhill
waiting so long for the rain.

The sandhill she paints is blue
just like the sea.
That's right.
Rain falls on a sandhill.
After being filtered,
it sinks deep under the ground.

I want to drink the water drops
under the ground.
Each drop—
How delicious it could be!
How soothing it could be!
I don't have her painting here.
But I know
it is the thirst of a sandhill
that she is looking at.
It is the underground lake of a sandhill
that she is looking at.

If I could swim there—
If I could touch the love there—
If I could look up at the sky there—
If I could enjoy the water drops,
each drop on my lip—

Earnestly, she is painting.
In the past, she was painting.
In the future, she will be painting.
The picture that touched my exhausted heart—
shall I go and see her again?

Leylouna

I repeat—
in the light
in the dark.
I go and return
again and again.

I don't know why.
I don't know for whom.

At that time
if you had not found me,
I would have been dead,
lost in the street.
I would have been dead
by the roadside.
Is it the ending that suits me?

In repeating,
I have been getting old.
Now I am blind.
If I hit something
I'll take the opposite direction.
If I feel something
I will freeze again.

Only your warmth
was my shelter.

My toes have worn out.
They are lukewarm.
Perhaps
it is the blood that bothers me.
Blind eyes give me
peace.

Since you found me
now I am here.

There is nothing
like the river of oblivion.

If my new toes come out
I will stop repeating and
I want to walk with you.

Blue Hourglass

I was watching the sand falling
again and again.
When all the sand fell,
I turned it over
again and again.
Still now.

It is not the time but something else
that I was watching.
I rolled it over.
I viewed it from the side.

The moment that I met you
the hourglass left behind
started to move again,
rustling,
as if I were watching the sea or clouds.
I lost myself in it for a long time.

It was the day before yesterday
that hourglass stopped for a while.
It changed from something being watched
to something watching us for a while.
Sticky body in the hot summer.
Rustling music.
My heart was beating at that time.

When the hourglass started to move again,
it was dark outside.
The singing of insects in early summer.
I was left alone
and played with the hourglass.
After talking with my precious friend,
I lay down my cleaned body.

The hourglass
at that time
and now
and in the future
—all the time.
It is watching us.
Not being watched by us.
That is the reality that I found.

From the Warm Place

I am watching outside from inside the room
warmed by the light of candles.
The ginkgo tree is scattering the leaves
that are completely yellow now.
The wind must be strong.
Businessmen are holding their coat collars
and hurrying home.

This café is rather fashionable
for a local one.
That's why it is not so crowded.
Taking off my down coat,
I order a café au lait and
I get some poetry out of my bag.

The music is modern with a strong low sound.
There is no one except a waitress.
Sitting down,
lighting a cigarette,
I turn the pages of the book.

It is the poetry that I want to read.
It is the poetry that I should read.
I am synchronized with the poetry,
captivated by it.

Many scenes appear in my mind.
Not scenes familiar to everyone,
but scenes that just pass away,
without being noticed.

Words thrill me,
the soft and tender mind of the author.
I thank him.

Still far away.
Not yet realized.
But let us do
whatever we can do.
Such phrases came to me.

Outside
housewives shop for today's dinner.
School boys ride bicycles.
I close the book
without knowing where I am.

Warm air encloses me,
leaving only hope.
I am about to lose myself
in the poetry.

It's the time when wintry blasts begin to blow.
Shall I go home now
with my shoulders hunched?

"Thank you."
"See you."
I just heard such a greeting.

A Rainbow at Night

A rainbow at night
shone with its color darker.
It's the first night rainbow I've seen.
The wound in my heart
melted away and
became
just like a warm sunny spot in daytime.

It is always true
that the night
brings us hope.
It whispers around the time,
crossing to tomorrow.

See? I said so.
It's alright.
Our hearts are connected.

On the way home
the moon cleaned my room.
Scattered clothes calmed down.

Slowly
the rainbow lured me to bed.

It was not seven colors.
The lights spread in my room
to enfold me.

It was more than a thousand lights.

Night Sea

Looking at the night sea,
looking at the waves of the night sea,
when I close my eyes,
I feel the depth of the night sea.

Following a wave
behind,
the endless drawing sound
tells how deep it is.

The endless wave following the sound
without any words
tells of human life and the life of the earth.

In this endless work
I saw myself
washed away by
eternity.

Universal Time

I hear the cries of the people
who are precious to me.

Silently,
I just write.

Even its meaning
I don't know.

At least I know there is someone
who wants to live.
By writing,
I was made to live.
By writing,
I have been soothed.

Even if it has no meaning,
this is the only thing
that I can do.
A sense of helplessness.
I can only feel saved
by writing.

Arrogant.
No sense of responsibility.
Perhaps a

tremendously
loveless way of life.

Yet, earnestly,
earnestly,
holding all the cries of the people,
this star
goes on
day by day.

Even though
I don't know your love,
still
the universe
enfolds us.

Someone may say
you are running away,
you are a loser.
But
I cannot help it.

Each of us
lives our life with all our strength.
One thing we can do is to pray,
only if there is a ray of light.

A Present

I had a dream.

In the transparent wind,
I lay down on a carpet of dandelions.
They were waving toward the blue sky.

Watching the flowing clouds,
I felt as if I were becoming transparent.

Closing my eyes,
I felt them
become hot,
then,
just like a child
hungry for love,
big tears
dropped from my eyes.

To me,
who wanted to be alone,
it was a present given by God—
me lying down on the carpet,
dandelions playing in the wind.

I was happy.
Warm sunlight

reflecting your smile
disappeared slowly.

What are you doing now?
Suddenly it ran through my mind.
Silent loneliness
came to me
who had wanted to be alone.

Then, from the dream,
I woke up.

Seeking Love

My own identity—
I didn't know it
even after the age of twenty.

Perhaps I was raised with love.
When I was a baby,
I think
my home was full of love.

At the age of two,
I kissed a boy at the public swimming pool.
Surprised, he started crying,
overturned in his float.
I was called "monster."
I just wanted to be a friend.

I ran after my teacher at kindergarten.
"She is the teacher for everyone."
I was pushed away.
I just wanted her to return my love.

At the age of five,
when I was in Paris because of my father's job,
I went to school with the school bag
I was proud of.

Someone shouted,
"Get your bag out of the way!"
On the way back home,
I was called
"Asian!" "Yellow!"

Coming back,
I entered Japanese school.
When I greeted the others,
they whispered,
"Gaijin!" "Alien!"
Still I wanted friends.

In primary school
I didn't want to go out.
I was pulling out my eyelashes,
stressed out,
lonely.

In junior high school,
suddenly I became popular.
"It's good to be mixed race, isn't it!"
"Cool!"
"I envy you!"
Confused,

I started to think
I didn't need to have friends.

I can't change so easily.
I don't know how to go on.

I found this at last when I went to America,
in the place where
individuals are respected.
I crouched down.
Who am I?
I groped for myself.
I lost my way.
I missed my way.
I collapsed.

When I realized
I was seeking love,
I relied on my mother again.
I clung to my father.
Regression at the age of twenty.
It has not been easy to identify myself.
That is why I have been writing,
That is the only thing I have.

But it is alright.
A part of me
that was not shaped
has stood up as a poem.
Though I cannot say anything great,
my voice from the heart can be heard.
I have found a place where I can be myself.

From there, my identity spreads.
When I eat the food of the Middle East,
I get excited.
When I talk with my good Japanese friends,
I can be happy.
When I am alone,
I have my poems.
Forever they are with me.
I want to think
that is enough.

Don't Cry Anymore

Since midnight
Squeak squeak
the squirrel cries.
Squeak squeak
Looking for friends,
it cries.
I heard,
"It's already spring."

Outside, the wind is cold.
Squeak squeak
However, the squirrel cries.
Squeak squeak
Once a year, they cry like this.
I heard,
"Friends are in the forest."

Tirelessly
Desperately
Squeak squeak
The squirrel has been crying.
Squeak squeak
Without eating, it cries.
I heard,
"I want my friends."

Don't cry anymore.
You have no friends here.
You should go further.
You can't find your friends here.
Can you live on
if I let you out of the cage?

Squeak squeak
Squeak squeak

The squirrel cries,
"I want to have friends."
"Just friends."

I Was There

In the early morning
when I could not sleep,
there was no one to hold me.

In the winter evening as the wind blew,
there was no one to warm me.

From the back seat of a car
I was just looking at the view.

I was just looking at the taller people
to read their facial expressions.

However, I found myself
inside of myself.

In the sleepless night,
in the madness,
I was looking at myself,
I held myself.

I was not alone,
I was not unloved.
Just
we were passing each other,
right?

I could bear the loneliness
in the early morning,
in the cold evening as the wind blew,
since
"you" were here.

"Me" in myself became "you"
who looked over me.

You have been looking over me
until today
and from now on.

Being loved by "you,"
I will live on.

II
Small World

The Hand You Hold

A pulse of love flowing through the hand you hold.
Feeling it, I was listening to
the song you sent.

Next to my mother sleeping quietly,
I was praying silently.

May my poor loved one find
a small happiness somewhere.
May the brave fighting with loneliness feel
a small peace.

To my loved one shedding tears with a broken heart,
may warm wind blow tenderly.

I love this hand full of love.
A feeling of appreciation leads me to tomorrow.

See you.
Take care.

Such an ordinary time
I want to feel together with you tonight.

Desire

Maybe someone has been wishing for a long time.
Country, People and Nature—
everything may be someone's wish.

Becoming generous by looking up at the blue sky—
becoming sweeter by looking at a baby—
lamenting for the reality that you found—
everything may be someone's wish.

If we are living on someone's wish,
just like an endless game we are playing,
then, it is rather easier to know the answer beforehand.
Why are we struggling to live?

Because I have been wishing continuously
since before I understood this,
even if it's an endless game with an unknown objective,
it may be that I wished to be as I am now.

Border

Because we are living in different places,
because we have different colors,
because we have different languages,
there is something that we cannot cross.

Not close enough to hold hands,
all the time passing each other,
losing heart to heart talk,
there is something that we cannot share.

Where are you from?
They were already decided when you were born,
the place you live and the color of your skin.

When did it come to be so?
Blinded by money,
people and society are coldhearted.

Because it is a different place,
because it is a different color,
because it is a different language—
that's exactly why we can understand each other,
that's exactly why we can consider each other.

What are you looking at?

A green line drawn on a map?
What are you thinking about?
The smile of that toothless boy on the TV?

Tell me
how far
is the border of our earth?

Grilled Fish

"Why do you always leave behind the grilled fish?"
I asked an old lady on the next bed in the hospital.
"You know, I cannot eat grilled fish."
Saying this, she looked out of the window.
"I see."
I thought all the elders liked fish.
I felt I asked something wrong.

She taught me how to wash and the way to shop at the hospital.
We had a long talk in the room.
She was a small old lady.

"Will you keep a secret? I don't want others to know it."
She started to talk.
"I was a nurse during the war.
There were many burned soldiers.
I cannot forget that smell.
It's the same smell as the grilled fish.
Nurses nowadays are elegant.
At the time, we were too busy to sleep."

Oh, that's why she cannot eat grilled fish.
I felt pain in my heart.
Nothing I know.
Her husband passed away.

Now she is alone.
"You know, we should never have war."
She was pricking a fish with chopsticks
so that it looked like it had been eaten.
I was imagining a shelter—
one after another injured soldiers being brought,
nurses working hard to take care of them,
soldiers dying, some dead.
How many times did she pray for them?
How many times did she pray for the end of the war?

"So, you are going to leave the hospital when the flowers bloom?
Why don't you come to my house? Let's pick horsetails together."
"Yes!" I happily replied.
How long had it been since my grandma died?
My grandma evacuated with my father during the war
waiting for grandpa who was captured in Siberia.

In the season of cherry blossoms
I visited her house as I promised.
A row of cherry trees from the bus stop.
A splendid fine day.
After praying to her husband at the household altar,
we picked horsetails together.
We talked for a long time.

We ate so many strawberries.
When I left,
she gave me horsetail tsukudani.
Waving her hands,
she said with a smile,
"Please come back again."

Thank you!
Of course, you cannot eat grilled fish.
Take care! I'll come back soon.
She secretly taught me what war is.
I felt pain, but was happy.

Blowing in the breeze of the evening,
cherry blossoms were falling.

Black Umbrella

It was fine in the morning.
I was comfortable
in a light laughter.
Someday, can I be just like that sky,
more and more transparent?
Such an idea lit my way.

Soon something will happen.
I cannot see it.
It is not clear yet.
But
something will happen.

It was cloudy in the afternoon.
The white rice in my lunchbox looked gray.
Can I see the sky just like in the morning?
Can I be like that sky?
I was deceiving myself.

Soon something will happen.
Not yet I know.
Not yet I feel.
But
something will happen

On my way home, it was raining.
My blue umbrella shed torrents of water.
Can I see the blue sky after the rain?
Can I see the most beautiful sky?
Such an idea was still in my mind.

Soon something will happen.
No one knows yet.
Not a single sign from the thermometer.
But
something will happen soon.

When I looked up at the sky,
my umbrella was black.
Raindrops running down my cheek
dropped silently,
full of the dirt of the world.

Under the Autumn Sky

Blowing in the gradually chilling wind,
with my mouth full of sandwich,
I am soaking in the music from my earphones
while watching the people walking by.

Today is the first day of a long holiday.
People are busy enjoying themselves.
An old man walks by with a stick.
I am feeling the "right now at this moment" of this country.

Flowing cars and buses,
laughing children in a car,
a child and a parent on a bicycle,
a woman taking a walk with a dog—
Yes, in this country, Japan,
I am sitting in the corner of this country
where people are taking peace for granted.

What would happen if a gunfight occurred here?
If we suddenly lost our lives with the drop of a bomb?
Peace would be broken in one breath,
just a shattered teen's dreams.

I do not hate this country.
I rather like this country.

Once I hated this country and left,
but I realized that this is my home.
That's why I want to protect this peace.

What can I do?
Where should I go?
I do not know.
However, I am happy now.
I am happy to see the people
who are enjoying their life.
I really appreciate
that I am beside them.

I don't know anything, but
I think I will keep on writing.

Thinking that
I cannot die,
I look at a father pushing a stroller.

I will not allow them to criticize us,
saying we are taking peace for granted.
These are the people who are really living in peace,
living in peace and quiet.
That's why I will not accept anything

which hurts this country deeply.
If such a thing happens,
I will survive.
I will survive to keep on writing.

Melody Invites Me to a Dream

The melody started just like a lullaby.
After taking a big breath,
a master made low sounds
quietly and softly.

Children slept in their beds,
smiling with the healing sounds
flowing on their smooth skin.
Adults shut their eyes and
remembered their childhood.

Tapping his toe to the rhythm,
the master lured us into the fantastic world.
Children crossed a bridge over the fish in the river.
Adults felt the wind on a great plain.

In a Romanian folk song
children fought against a dragon,
adults danced with a dreamlike partner.

The master kept time with his whole body.
The high-pitched sound trembled.

Children now saved the kingdom by defeating the dragon.
Adults now opened their eyes and picked apples.

Suddenly the tune changed.
The master twanged vigorously.
Everyone in the hall was united and the climax came.
At a great cheer from the audience,
the master bowed deeply with an air of satisfaction.
A big bouquet and another bow.

Now the melody stays in our memory.
Holding each of our dreams,
we go outside into the wind.

A Healing Land

Cafés line the coast of the multinational country.
People eat while speaking many languages.
Like blackbirds,
surfers ride the waves
a little far away.
White birds are in the blue sky,
enjoying their own vacation.

The place gathers people,
attracts people
with its beautiful landscape.
Like a hot crush in the daytime,
it intoxicates people.

In the evening,
lighted candles here and there,
people gather to see the sun
going down in the sea.
Palm trees create shadows.
The shining sea peeps through the trees
again tonight
like a secret disclosed.
It intoxicates people a little.

At night,
a little waning moon up in the sky.

In the sea,
the moon also appears and
gathers people.
Now is the time for lovers to kiss each other.
The city collects the scenes for the postcards.
Just by the sound of the waves
the sea takes lovers with it.
Slowly it turns into terror-like black.
Again it intoxicates people.

At midnight
there are no people,
just the sky and the sea stretching their arms.
Exchanging words of care and love,
silently holding this star,
like they have been
since the time they were born,
they issue the color of blue.

Early in the morning, birds are singing.
Joggers appear
alongside vagrants out getting their breakfast.
Cafés will open soon to gather people
with the aroma of espresso.
Sleepy tourists will take a late breakfast,
watching the sea with a map.

Hiding the wounds of the people,
the place has been a healing land.
Now it becomes crowded and noisy.
With the blessing of sky and sea,
the place has started its day again.

"Never End" - The Promise Given?

What was the promise given at that time?
All Japan was dyed with the songs made by Komuro Tetsuya.
There was a phenomena called "Amura~."
Amuro Namie, the most popular singer.

Falling ill,
I came back from the US where I had gone to study.
After falling ill,
I visited Okinawa with my mother for the first time.
It was the off season of April.
Blue sky and blue sea,
much bluer than in mainland Japan.

We drove to the hotel near the site of the Summit.
I was holding the wheel
recovering a little from the illness,
full of hope
as I had been in California.

At the hotel of huge pillars,
I sat on the big sofa with my mother
enjoying iced café au lait.
The waitress was a student from France.
We had a good talk.
Slowly,

very slowly,
time passed.

Thinking that man is coming here,
I was also thinking about
the meaning of the song "Never End,"
observing myself living in this age.
I was asking,
is it okay to leave it as "Never End"?

Amuro Namie sang the song at the Summit.
Our future will never end.
Our tomorrow will never end.
Supported by endless sweetness
Wind blows with unforgettable memories.

Did they understand the song?
"Never End" is not the relationship of the two countries,
but it is the wound that Okinawa had and still has, isn't it?
Japanese virtue wants to think everything is okay,
the coward way of thinking.
Did those men understand that?

Small World

You know, they say that the world is small.
Perhaps it is true.
You know, they say that if you wish, it will be realized.
Perhaps it is true.
We are connected
and our wishes will be realized.

Someone realizes someone else's wish.
We share prayers, sadness and happiness.
They say it is globalization.
Deeper than words,
we may be connected deep in our minds,
being synchronized.

That is why
if the sadness is big
it will expand.
We should stop it
before it makes a sea of tears.
Never ever.
No more sacrifice.
We should pray
from the bottom of our hearts.
You know.
From the bottom of our hearts.

The Flower Called Haya

This flower has no thorns.
She came flying with the wind.

Accepting her fate,
thinking of her homeland all the time,
this flower kept praying for
the flowers broken by the strong wind
and the flowers stamped down miserably.

Blooming in a land far away from home,
with a strong belief,
increasing her petals,
she has grown up as a big flower
and started to send
what she has
to her home,
to the small "Flowers of Hope" left behind at home.

A petal for the flower which lost one.
A stem for the flower which lost one.

Haya helped them fully bloom.
She has made them in full bloom.

Now other flowers have begun to ask,

"What can I do for them?"
And they also have begun to give
their own petals and stems.

The flower called Haya
became larger and larger.

Other flowers shared her belief in tears.
With the great help of other flowers,
finally
she has accomplished what she wished.

Crossing over the border
with the help of the wind,
Haya sent her abundant love
to the flowers which lost their stems and petals.

At home
the "Flowers of Hope" started to bloom
here and there,
making colorful gardens
facing Haya.

The name of Haya will be remembered.
But that is not Haya's wish.

Haya just wanted
to help other flowers find what is happening in the world,
so that the flowers of hope will not be injured anymore.

Haya's prayer will spread
to the world
with her seeds flying
on the wind.

Until no more flowers are hurt
in this world,
the flower will bloom gloriously.

III

A Sunny Spot

Solitary Evening

Before the quiet night falls,
feeling the burning sun on my back,
I hold the agony-like feeling.
Why do we want love?
Why do we want to be loved?

Searching for my meaning to exist,
hearing the loud buzz of cicadas in my mind,
this evening, I feel emptiness.
The people that I saw yesterday,
the people that I am going to see today—
do I want love even from the people passing by?

I have been waiting for this time.
When all the people who disappear into the dark
are ready for sleep,
I feel sorry for myself
who is awake.

I am awake asking these questions.
I feel sorry for myself.
Why do we want love?
Why do we want to be loved?

I ease myself
by thinking that
I am unhappy.
That misapprehension
visits me tonight again.
Should I love
this pain
this delusion?

I want to sleep nestled up to my mother
just like a baby who doesn't know anything.
I'm scared to be rejected in this illusion.
Why do we want love?
Why do we want to be loved?

As I looked for the answer in vain,
evening came again.
In the faint buzz of cicadas
I am feeling the summer.

The Lace of My Heart

My heart is white lace
knit by my mother.

One switch, one switch—
she knitted carefully,
fragile but soft.

I can't remember when it was.
It got a hole and
from the hole,
the lace became loose.
Before she knew it,
there was a larger hole.

My mother tried to fix it
in a hurry,
but it never became as it once was.

It's because I gave my heart
to someone else,
not to my mother.

Sorry, Mom.
I'll knit my lace myself.

It may be different from the first one
but I'll try to make it beautiful.

Don't cry, Mom.
Don't worry, Mom.

It might not be like the one
which is popular
but—

My heart is a white lace
knit by my mother.

Fragile but soft.

Wrapping a loose thread around my finger,
slowly I rest it on my chest.

The Crisis

The hot water in the bathtub is swaying,
transparent, smooth, and somehow heavy.
The discolored manicure on my toes sways with it.
This morning,
my father passed the crisis.

In the sickroom, my father and I listened to
the music of "Recuerdos de la Alhambra,"
sharing the earphones.
He said, "It releases my mind."
What I could do was just pray silently that
he could enjoy writing poems and essays again.

It's usually noisy and bothersome,
but today
I thanked everyone in the room.
I was able to talk with him
eye to eye
before he leaves for the endless journey.

Just two boiled eggs for my supper tonight.
I didn't feel like going out for my supper.
From the slightly open window
I heard cars crashing through the rain.

Tomorrow will be a different day.
His painful breathing rings in my ears.
Trying to sleep,
I'm in a dream-like space
in a distant place.
I feel like I have been on a long journey
to somewhere.

A Heartbeat

Oil-flavored zippo.
In order to keep a peaceful mind,
my father was polishing the silverware
silently.

I heard that
he often bathed me
when I was a child.

I often heard him
sing a chanson
from the bathroom
when I was growing up.

I was a girl
but played catch,
putting on the baseball glove.
In a park,
I fell over and over.
He taught me how to ride a bicycle.
We enjoyed cycling on the riverside road.
In the summer holidays,
we climbed Yatsugatake.
I troubled him.
I was poor at mountain-climbing.

Living separately,
we often quarreled.
I sometimes hated him

He was suffering from his chronic complaint.
He wrote "spacewalk"
on his oxygen tank.

On the day I saw my father off,
I cried madly.

My father frantically struggled to live.

Throb, throb, throb…

I feel him beside me.
He is guiding me.
Here am I who never stops writing.

Well-polished zippo
Flickering flame
in the dark.

Throb…

Basking in My Father's Love

I woke up
before the birds started to sing,
on a silent and chilly morning.

At last I managed to be here.
My father seemed to have been waiting for me,
I felt calm and quiet.

A huge amount of books,
his memorabilia.
What shall I do with them?

Now I just want to
treasure the time with him
over a cup of instant coffee
feeling the brightening light from the outside.

He is here.
He is there.
He is in myself
and in those who remember him.

Birds' song.
I feel his heartbeat.
Here I am,

miserable,
full of regrets.
He is watching me warmly.

I will watch you all the time!
From heaven,
from earth,
I don't know from where.
But now,
he is watching
everything of me.

I wonder if
the chain of life will bring
meaning to human beings.
I cannot do anything bad!
I say to myself bashfully.

A model of a red sports car
I bought for him in New York.
He displayed it
together with my picture.

In the morning twilight,
birdsong gained its power,

ready for the start of the day.

The Japanese red pine
stands silently
and breathes on
the central pillar.
Now it has lost him.

But
the house has not lost its master.
It rather makes him live in it.
Feeling that way
I gained another memory of him.

Aroma

The night I visited my mother in the hospital
I could not sleep till midnight.
Just listening to piano music,
I was looking at the photo of my father
on the table by the sofa.

His face was soft,
looking at me with his warm eyes.
I cannot believe he is not here.
He just went out for a short trip.

The cats could not sleep either and
played with some balls.
Comfortable music through earphones.
I remembered the movie "Porco Rosso"
that I saw with my father many times.

When it is time for my mother to wake up,
the nurse will take her temperature.
She will ask how many times she woke up for the toilet.
She will slowly stand up with sleepy eyes.
Papa, Mama fell over.
Be with her, it hurts.

Outside
it grew brighter from the darkness.
There came an aroma of lavender
floating with the piano music.

Alone in the Hospital

In the evening as it grows dark,
alone on a bench outside a hospital,
looking at the green,
my mother is listening to birds' songs.

She must be the only foreigner in the hospital.
Everybody is kind to her,
but I know my mother still feels lonely.

I wish I could visit her every day.
If I could,
I would not leave her alone.
She talks and laughs
about the chocolate she got at the store,
about the nurse who has her own car.

"You are great, Mama."
"Taking on the power of nature, you are finding your own way."

Greens and birds' songs are soothing to her.
It's only a little bit more
until she can go home.

A Bipedal Walking Green Hand

The wind is blowing through the hole in my mind.
It increases its burning pain.
The wound has opened wide.
I don't know how to treat it.

I was on the shoulder of my father
laughing loudly.
I was in the chest of my mother
sleeping peacefully.
Were they hundreds of millions of years ago?

Since then,
I have aged more than 30 years.
The memory is now swept away into oblivion.
I miss my father's gnarled hands.
I miss my mother's soft chest.
Since when
have I been walking on two legs?

A wound which cannot be cared for.
Love devoted to someone in vain.
Wanting to be loved and now
there is no other way than
just giving my love to my cats.
I am living
a self-satisfied life.

I want to hear you.
I want to touch you.
I want to be embraced
with the words "I love you."
Sway me to the place,
to the place under the warm sunlight,
to the place where I can hear the breathing of
my father and mother.

Since I am not used to walking on two legs,
I trip over the same stone
again and again.
The hole in my mind has not yet been covered.
But someday
when you come back from oblivion,
that may be the time
when I can stand with my two legs,
firm and steady.

Memory of Being Wild

When the cat stares at the wind,
the footprints of the ancestors
disappear, dancing with the sand.

On the dead tree branch,
leaving the littered remains of the meat,
it dreams.

The sun goes down.
The cat squinches its eyes.
The past stares at me with fixity.

A part of the wildness
urges the balance of the mind.
The lying lissome figure
makes me feel the unknown world
closer to me.

The footprints left in the past,
something that danced down,
now fixing my eyes to the future.
I take the first step silently.

With Someone Somewhere

The cat's teeth,
small but sharp,
love bite my toe.
Sweet enough not to hurt,
it is fawning and licking with its tongue.

Enjoying the peace given by these little cats
who were ripped away from their mother after just a month,
I am irritated that I cannot be their mother.
Do they notice it?

The eyes looking at me uncomfortably—
melancholy faces
and curious expressions.
All things should be watched by their mother,
not by me.

Coming across them,
welcoming them as family members—
we are exchanging our love,
giving and receiving,
though uneasily.

Somewhere in the world
there is a boy with a gun.

There are adults who teach him how to shoot.
Even though he has a family
he cannot see their smile,
he cannot share the smile and
happiness with his family.

Just right now
there is a child who was ripped away from his mother
and there is a mother who is crying.
On my lap
a kitten mews,
staring at me.

Somewhere somewhere
Someday someday
Someone someone—
By connecting
not in the form of fight
but in the form of family,
I wish they could soothe
their minds in this world.

A Sunny Spot

There is a soft sunny spot
on the bed
on an early spring afternoon.
Rubbing the cat's fur with my fingers,
I feel its heart beating
with my eyes closed.

They hate to be held
but they like to lie down on the bed.
They cuddle close to me,
like they can share my pain.

The light out of the window
shines on us
making quiet happiness in this house.
I feel the love wrapped in the warmth,
just like that day.

The cats accept my fingers.
I pat them with full love.
As you did to me,
I want to give peace to them.
The lace curtain sways.
Each of us dreams our own dream.

It may just be temporary, but—
I feel the most happiness in this moment.
I taste slowly
this season
this heartbeat
thinking
it may be love
that I am feeling now.
My thoughts go around.

Cats sleep on my lap
in endless comfort.
The sunny spot disappeared,
leaving loneliness behind.

For just a moment
in the warmed room
I had a dream with my cats.
Your back,
just like that time,
was retreating far away,
and I woke up
clutching a cat's back.

Shedding warm tears

on my pillow,
I stood up and
smiled to the cats
looking at me out of the blanket.
Thanks to them,
my tears lessened.

Whatever happens
you should be positive.
It was my resolution for this year.
Repeating it in my mind,
I head toward the kitchen for coffee,
leaving behind the disappeared sunny spot and my cats on a bed.

Strong feelings of "We are connected beyond the sea."

Maya Inoue A book of poetry in English and Japanese: *Small World*

Hisao Suzuki

Maya Inoue is a poet who has already published four books of poetry and one poetry art book. Her fourth book was awarded the Prize of the 50th Yokohama Poets Association. Her books are highly evaluated by poetry critics. Thirty-four poems out of the past five books are translated into English in this book, together with the Japanese version. Ms. Inoue was born in Yokohama to a Syrian-French mother and a Japanese father. Her mother is a native speaker of French and also a fluent speaker of English. Her late father, Teruo Inoue, was a scholar of French and also a well-known poet. Therefore, she must have been talking with her parents not only in Japanese but also in French and English. In other words, they were connected through three languages; but for this book, she asked a poet and a scholar of English, Keiko Yonaha, to translate her poems into English since her native tongue is Japanese. She wanted to have her relatives and friends in France and the U.S. read her poems. I think she also wanted to have more people in the world, not just those in Japan, read her poems. This book consists of three chapters: Chapter 1, "Tooriame" (A Passing Shower); Chapter 2, "Small World"; and Chapter 3, "Hidamari" (A Sunny Spot). Let me quote the first three stanzas from the poem "Tooriame" in the first chapter.

Standing under the roof / during a passing shower / in early summer / I smell the dust / thrown up by the rain. / / Greens may be happy now. / Flowers and plants, / rice fields and vegetable fields— / all may be happy now. / / People are busy looking for roofs and umbrellas. / But rain is necessary for Nature. / It is strange / that we are living together.

We feel her subtle sensitivity in the Japanese poem "Tooriame." The first stanza describes a scene in which in the fine blue sky of early summer, suddenly rain clouds gather and the rain started to fall on the dry soil. The author escapes under a roof and waits for the rain stop. Then, the dust thrown by the rain comes up to her and she smells it. This scene reminds me of a picture of Ukiyoe, "Niwaka ame" (A shower), and she brings us to the world of "Tokaido Gojyu San tugi" drawn by Utagawa Hiroshige. She remarkably expresses Japanese people's sensitivity from cultivating a life enjoying the changes in Nature. However, she also reminds us that it is wrong to limit such sensitivity only to Japanese people; she suggests that this kind of sensitivity also exists in every person, everywhere in the world. In the second stanza, she says, "Greens may be happy now." She shares not the feeling of the people trying to avoid the rain, but the feeling of the plants. Realizing the gap in the feeling toward the rain between the humans and the plants, she whispers, "It is strange that we are living together." Ms. Inoue is a poet who cannot help but feel the wonder of the coexistence of humans and plants, since she can understand the feelings of both. Ms. Yonaha translated her sensitivity skillfully, adding the hidden subject with the rhythm of English. The poem asks us the fundamental question, how can we humans live a sustainable life by taking back respect for Nature, in a situation in which the global environment is being destroyed by humans' egoistic economic activity? I believe the answer to that question lies in the sensitivity described in Ms. Inoue's poem. It is important for us to take back such sensitivity. She tells us that the sensitivity in the poem "Small World" can change the world. I'd like to finish this brief commentary by quoting the first stanza in the poem "Small World."

You know, they say that the world is small. / Perhaps it is true. / You know, they say that if you wish, it will be realized. / Perhaps it is true. We are connected / and our wishes will be realized.

This strong feeling of "We are connected" lies in the mind of Ms. Inoue, who created a *Small World* and this feeling will be the spirit of her poetry and the motive of her writing. That is what I felt reading this poetry. I'd like you to read these thirty-four poems full of her fresh sensitivity.

POSTSCRIPT

First of all, I'd like to thank you for having read my first book of poetry in English and Japanese. Though I had been thinking about publishing my poetry in a language other than Japanese, I was not able to get the chance. This time, thanks to Mr. Hisao Suzuki, the head of the publisher Coal Sack, I came to know Ms. Keiko Yonaha, a poet, an English teacher, and an interpreter, and my long-time dream was at last realized. Since I have been writing the poems only in Japanese so far, I heard that my mother was often asked by my foreign relatives and friends, "What is Maya writing?" I'm really happy that these people close to me can read my poems now. For this book, Mr. Suzuki edited it and commented on it, and Ms. Yonaha translated my Japanese into English. I appreciate their devotion from the bottom of my heart. On the cover of the book, you can see a picture of my mother in her youth and me in my childhood. The picture was taken by my late father. I can see the three of us in the picture and certainly we lived in a "small world" made up by the three of us. That was my starting point. I learned various things from my parents inside of it, and from it, I saw the outer world. Now, it can be said that we are living in a "small world," a so called information-oriented world. Without realizing it, we are living in it, learning in it, and seeing the outer world from it. If all the people in the world imagine a peaceful world in their mind and heart by wishing the happiness of other people, then this world will be a small world full of happiness. If they just fight each other or blame each other, then this world will be a small world, just cramped and uncomfortable. The Internet and free calling have made the world very convenient. While I appreciate it, I'd like to pray for the people who are hurt by the tragedies still occurring in the world. The poem "The Flower Called Haya" was dedicated to my second cousin, Haya, who emigrated from Syria to the U.S. When she entered UCLA, she established an NPO to provide artificial arms and legs to Syrian children and the people who lost their arms and legs in the civil war. It drew media attention, and the movement that she started has been growing. Moved by her passion, and to convey her wishes and prayers for the people to many more people, I wrote the poem for her.

I'm delighted if this poem can touch someone's heart and help them to share her wish. I don't know what kind of book this poetry will be for you, but I'm just happy if you enjoy the poems not only in Japanese, but also in English, and I'm happier if this poetry can leave something in your heart.

Maya Inoue, December 2019

Author's brief history

Maya Inoue

Maya was born to a Syrian-French mother and a Japanese father in Yokohama, Japan, in 1976. Having lived in Japan, France, and the U.S., she had a difficult time identifying herself. She studied theater art and started to write poems on the internet and in the literary magazine *COAL SACK*. Her father, Teruo Inoue (1940 – 2015) was a poet and a scholar of French literature. She republished his work *Saint Simeon's Horned Owl: A Trip to Syria and Lebanon* (Midnight Press).

Published Works:

Poetry: *Look at Me—Tatoebanashi—* (Midnight Press)
Poetry: *Leylouna-Hakanai Ai no Tatoebanashi* (Midnight Press)
Poetry: *Yami no Honoo* (Coal Sack)
Poetry: *Kodo* (Coal Sack) the 50th Yokohama Poets Association Prize
English and Japanese Poetry: *Small World* (Coal Sack)
Art and Poetry, with Kamutsuki ROI: *Particulier—Kokkyo no Saki he* (Coal Sack)

Address: 227-0043, 2-37-2 Fujigaoka, Aoba-ku, Yokohama-shi, Greenhill b-302

石炭袋

Maya Inoue 『SMALL WORLD』
A Collection of Poems in English and Japanese
井上摩耶 英日詩集 『スモールワールド』

2020 年 1 月 18 日　初版発行

著　者　　　　井上　摩耶
訳　者　　　　与那覇恵子
編集・発行者　鈴木比佐雄
発行所　　　　株式会社 コールサック社

〒 173-0004　東京都板橋区板橋 2-63-4-209
電話 03-5944-3258　FAX 03-5944-3238
suzuki@coal-sack.com　http://www.coal-sack.com
郵便振替 00180-4-741802
印刷管理　（株）コールサック社　制作部

装丁　奥川はるみ

落丁本・乱丁本はお取り替えいたします。
ISBN978-4-86435-426-4　C1092　￥2000E

Coal Sack Publishing Company
2-63-4-209 Itabashi Itabashi-ku Tokyo 173-0004 Japan
Tel: (03) 5944-3258 / Fax: (03) 5944-3238
suzuki@coal-sack.com　http://www.coal-sack.com
President: Hisao Suzuki

目次

井上摩耶　英日詩集

スモールワールド

I章　通り雨

通り雨

土の匂いが舞い上がる
初夏の通り雨
屋根のあるところから
そっと感じている

緑がよろこぶだろうな
花が野が
田んぼが畑が
よろこぶだろうな

人は傘や屋根を探すけれど
自然には不可欠な雨
なんだか不思議
共存していることが

桜が散って
銀杏が芽吹く
グラデーションのように
変化して行く人の心のように……

私の心の中にも大地があるなら
香っているのだろうか？
この土の匂いのような
柔らかい力強い香りが

アスファルトが濡れてゆき
猫は居眠り
私は少し窓を開けて
香りを楽しんでいる

ハトが遠くでクルックーと鳴いた

6

砂丘を描く女性

いつからか永遠に砂丘を描いている女性がいる

砂丘に魅了され　それ以来ありとあらゆる砂丘を巡り

砂を持って帰って来ては　絵具に混ぜて描く

何メートルも何メートルも…

何故そこまで砂丘に魅せられたのか？

一瞬も同じ時がないからだと

その波紋も美しいけれど　すぐに消えてしまうと

言っていた

私はその女性が好きだ

いつまでもいつまでも　時には何時間も

砂丘を描き続ける姿を思うと力強い

どこか凛とした女性を感じる

しかし　私の今の心は　砂丘の表面のように乾いていて

ずっとずっと　雨が降るのを待っているかのようだ

彼女の描く砂丘は蒼い　まるで海でもあるかのように

そう　砂丘にも雨は降り　ろ過されて地下深くへと沈水

する

私はその地下で　一滴一滴落ちて来る水滴を　飲みたい

どんなにおいしいことか　どんなに心が潤うことか

ここに彼女の絵はない

しかし　私にはわかる　彼女は砂丘の渇きだけを見てい

るのではないと

なぜなら　その蒼い砂丘の絵からは　地下の湖まで見え

るからだ

そこで泳ぎたいな

そこで愛に触れたいな

そこで空を見てみたいな

一滴一滴落ちて来る水滴に　唇濡らしたいな

彼女はひたすら描く

今までも　これからも

私の渇いた心に触れる絵だ

また逢いに行こうか…

レイルーナ

私は繰り返す
光の中を
闇の中を
繰り返し行ったり来たりする

何のためかはわからない
誰のためかもわからない

あの時
あなたが見つけてくれなかったら
私は死んでいただろう
路頭に迷って
野垂れ死に
私には、お似合い？

繰り返す中で
少しずつ老廃して
私は目が見えなくなった
何かにぶち当たれば
反対方向へ

何かを感じれば
また固まって

あなたの暖かさだけが
私の隠れ家だった
足の指は擦り切れて
生暖かい
多分
血液が私を悩ます
見えない目は
私に安らぎを…

あなたが見つけてくれたから
今 私はここにいる

忘却の川なんて
そんなものはない

私は繰り返すのをやめて
足の指がまたはえたら
あなたと歩きたい

8

青い砂時計

砂時計の砂が落ちて行くのを何度となく眺めては　また
ひっくり返して
その繰り返しをずっとずっとやって来た気がする　今も
まだ…

青い砂がサラサラと落ちて行くのを見るのは時間ではな
い何か
時には転がしてみたり
時には斜めから見てみたり

あなたと出逢った瞬間　置き去りにされた砂時計がまた
動き始めた
サラサラ　サラサラ
まるで海でも　雲でも見ているかのように
ボーッと　ずーっと

その砂時計が一昨日一時停止した　少しの時間私たちを
見守る側に…
暑い日のべたっとする身体　サラサラと流れる音楽

あの時私の心は息をしていた

また砂時計が動き始めた頃　外は夕暮れ　初夏の虫の声
私は一人置いてきぼりになって
転がって砂時計と遊ぶ
大切な友人に連絡をしてから　キレイになった身体で横
たわる

この砂時計はいつだって　あの時から　これからだって
ずっと
私が見ているようで　本当は私たちを見守っている

暖かい場所から

ロウソクの灯った暖かい空間から外を眺めていた
目の前にはすっかり黄色くなった銀杏の木が葉を散らし
ていて
風が強いのか仕事帰りのサラリーマンがコートの襟に手
をやる

このカフェレストランは地元にしてはずいぶんお洒落で
そのせいかいつも空いている
ダウンを脱ぐとアイスカフェオレを頼みカバンから詩集
を取り出した

音楽は現代的で低音を強めていて
店には従業員以外私一人であった
そこでゆったり座り込みタバコに火を付けると私は詩集
のページをめくり出した

活字離れしたとはいえ読みたい詩集であったし
読まなければいけないとも思っていた
その第一篇から私は吸い込まれるように音楽とともにそ

の世界観へとシンクロした

情景が、あちこちで思いを巡らせた光景が浮かぶ
決して皆が見たことのない光景ではないのだか
ただ多くの人は見逃して何も感じないで通り過ぎてしま
う風景

時々出て来るドキッとする言葉
柔らかくて優しい作者の心
そういったものに触れて私はまたふと感謝した

―遠いねぇ―
―まだだねぇ―
―でもやれるだけやってみようよ―
そんな声が心を駆け抜けた

外を見れば夕飯の買い出しから帰る主婦や
自転車を飛ばす学生
私は自分の立ち位置がわからないまま詩集を閉じた

暖かい空間は私を包み

希望を残して詩集の中へ消えて行きそうだった

そろそろ木枯らし
背中丸めて帰ろうか

—ありがとう—
—また来てね—
そんな声を聞いた

夜の虹

夜にかかる虹は色を濃くして光った
この世に産まれ初めて見た夜の虹

昼間の暖かな日だまりみたいになった
心の傷みはスーっと溶けてなくなり

いつもそうだ夜は希望をもたらす
明日という時間を越えた頃そっと囁く

〈ね？言ったでしょう？大丈夫だって〉
〈心は繋がってるよ〉って

帰り道に見た月が部屋の中の空気をキレイにして
散らかった服達が静まる時間となる

虹は確かにかかっていて少しずつ私をベッドへと誘う

夜の虹は良く見ると七色ではなくて
部屋中に広がり私を包んだ

まるで千色をも越える光りで

夜の海

夜の海を見て
夜の海の波を見て
夜の海の波を見て
目を閉じた時
夜の海の深さを感じる

ひと波の後ろへ続く
その果てしない
すい込まれていくような音は
何より海の深さを語る

あとにかぶさる
終わることのない波は
一言も加えることなく
人の人生を、地球の歩みを語る

私は永遠のその働きの中で
なぜかそれにさらわれていく自分を見た

宇宙時間

私の大切な人たちの
心の悲鳴が聞こえる

声も出さずに
私はただ「書く」

その意味すらわからないのだけれど

「生きよう」とする誰かがいることもわかっているから

私は「書く」ことで
「生かされて」
「書く」ことで
「癒されて」

意味がなくとも
それしかできない
無力感と
書いている自分を

「救われた」と
思うしかできなくて

傲慢で
無責任で
もしかしたら
とほうもなく
愛のない生き方かもしれない

それでもひたすら
ひたすら
みなの心の悲鳴を
この星は包み込み
一日を進めてゆく

私に
あなたの思いがわからなくとも
宇宙だけは
私たちを包んでくれている

それを

「逃げ」と
「負け」と
ステッカーを貼られても
そこだけは
もうどうにもならない

それぞれが
必死に「生きる」
一筋の光があればと
願うしかできないのだから

プレゼント

夢を見た

透き通った風の中で
横たわる私がいて
一面のタンポポが
青空に向かって揺れている

流れていく雲を
じっと　眺め
自分がどんどんキレイになる
そんな気持ちになった

しばらく目を閉ざしていたら
知らないうちに目が熱くなって
まるで愛に飢えた子供のように
大粒の涙が　こぼれ落ちた

一人になりたいと願った私に
神様がくれたプレゼント

そこに横たわる私と
風と遊ぶタンポポたち

幸せだった
暖かな陽射しが
あなたの笑顔を映して
ゆっくりと消えていった

「今頃　何をしてる?」
ふっとよぎった想いが
一人になりたいと願った私に
静かなさみしさを呼んだ

こうして　目が覚めた

14

愛を求め続けて

自分のアイデンティティなんて
二十歳を超えてもわからずにいた

多分愛されて育った
社会を知らない赤ちゃんの時
家庭は愛に溢れていた気がする……

二歳の時　公共のプールで男の子にキスをした
相手がビックリして泣き出して
浮輪ごとひっくり返った事件があった
友だちになりたかっただけなのに
「モンスター！」と叫ばれた

幼稚園に入り先生を追いかけ回した
「先生はみんなの先生！」と
突き放された……
愛情を返して欲しかっただけなのに

五歳　父の仕事でパリに住んでいた時

自慢のランドセルで学校へ行ったら
「邪魔だよこれ！」と毎回言われた
帰り道「アジア人！黄色い外国人！」とも言われた

帰国して日本の学校へ入った
初日　挨拶のために前へ出ると
「外人！宇宙人！」と言われた
寂しかった……
それでも私はまだ友達が欲しかった……

小学校中学年
私はおもてに出たくなくなった
ストレスでまつ毛を抜いていた

中学校
急に人気者になった
「ハーフってなんかいいよね！」
「かっこいい！」
「羨ましい！」
私は混乱した
友達なんていらないって思いはじめた

15

小さな居場所を見つけた

そこから広がる自分のアイデンティティ
中東料理を食べれば血がうずくし
気の合う日本人の友達と話すと楽しい
一人でいる時　私には詩がある
ずっとずっと寄り添ってくれる
それでいいんだと思いたい

そんなに上手く波乗りなんて出来ないよ
渡米してわかった
個々が尊重される環境で
私はうずくまる思いだった
「私は誰?」
模索した　迷った　道を踏み外した
崩壊した

気づけばまた愛を求め母にすがった
父に甘えた
二十歳にして赤ちゃんからやり直し
アイデンティティの形成はそう簡単ではなかった
だから書き続けた
それしか残っていなくて……

でもそれでよかった
ずっと形にならなかった私の一部が
「詩」として立ち上がったから
偉そうな事は言えなくても
心の声は聞いてもらえる

もう泣かないで

夜中からずっと

カウ　カウ

と　リスが鳴いている

カウ　カウ

と　友達を捜して鳴く

もう春ですね

そんな声を聞いた

外にでれば　風は冷たい

カウ　カウ

それなのに　リスは鳴く

カウ　カウ

年に一度　こうして鳴く

友達は森に居ますよ

そんな声を聞いた

休みなく　必死に

カウ　カウ

と　ずっと鳴いている

カウ　カウ

と　餌を食べずに鳴く

友達をください

そんな声を聞いた

もう泣かなくていいよ

だってここには友達いないもの

もっと遠くへ行かなきゃ

見つからないもの

籠から出したら　生きてゆけるの？

カウ　カウ

カウ　カウ

リスは友達が欲しいと

ただそれだけだと　鳴く

17

私がいた

眠れぬ早朝に
抱きしめてくれる人はいなかった

木枯らしの夕方に
コートをかけてくれる人もいなかった

車の後部座席から
ただただ景色を眺めるだけのドライブ

自分よりずっと背の高い人の
顔色を窺う日々

そう思ってきたけれど
私には「私」がいた

眠れぬ夜も
狂気の中でも
「私」は私を見つめ
抱きしめてくれていた

一人なんかじゃないんだ
愛されていなかったわけではないんだ
ただ少しすれ違っていただけ
そうでしょう？

早朝の
木枯らしの夕暮れの
寂しさに耐えてこられたのも
きっと「あなた」がいたから

私の中の「私」が「あなた」となって
ずっとずっと私を見守ってきた

今までも
これからも……

私は「あなた」に愛され
生き抜いていく

II章　スモールワールド

つないだ手

つないだ手から流れる愛情の脈

それを感じながら聴いていた

送られてきた歌を

私は静かに祈っていた

静かに寝入る母の隣で

どこかで悲しむ私の愛する人が

小さな幸せを見つけることが出来るように

孤独と戦う勇者が小さな安らぎを感じることが出来るように

ひび割れた心に涙する私の愛する人のそばに

そっと暖かな風が吹くようにと

私は、この愛情に満ちた手が大好き

この時
感謝する気持ちが私を明日へとつなぐ

さようなら。
またね。
元気でね!

そんな当たり前を
今夜はあなたと感じたい

望み

ずっと望んでいたのかもしれない
国も　民族も　自然も
今ある全ては　誰かの望みかもしれない

青空を見て　寛大になれるのも
赤ちゃんを見て　優しくなれるのも
現実を知って　嘆くのも
そんな全てが　誰かの望みかもしれない
私達が　誰かの望みで生きているのなら
まるで結末のわからないゲームをしているようで
それならば　いっそのこと　答えを見てしまえば楽なの
に
どうしてこんなに一生懸命
生きているのか　私達は

望み続けてきたから
知らないうちに　人生の目的が
結末のわからないゲームでも
今の私が
今の私を望んでいるのかもしれない

国境

住むところが違うから
肌の色が違うから
話す言葉が違うから
わかり合えない　何かがある

手と手をつなぐに至らなくて
いつも　すれ違いを繰り返して
心と心の　会話が減っていく
わかり合えない　何かがある

どこから来たのか
生まれた時に決められた
自分の生きる場所と　肌の色

いつから始まったのか
札束のために　目をむき出す
人間味のない　人と社会

知らない土地だから
違う肌の色だから

わからない言葉だから

それだからこそ　わかり合える
お互いを　思いやれる

あなたは何を見ているの
地図に書かれた　緑の上の直線？
あなたは何を考えているの
テレビに映される　歯のないあの子の笑顔？

私に教えて
どこまでが
この地球の国境なの？

焼き魚

「ねえ、どうしていつも焼き魚だけ残すの？」
入院中隣のベッドだったおばあちゃんに聞いた
「私ね、焼き魚たべられないのよ……」
そう言ってそっと窓の外を見た
年輩の方は魚が好きだと思っていた私は、少し悪いこと
を聞いたかなと思った
「そうなんだ……」

入院してすぐ洗濯の仕方や、売店を案内してくれたお
ばあちゃん
部屋に居る時は良く話した
身体の小さいおばあちゃんだった

「内緒にしてくれる？　みんなには知られたくないの」
そう言って話し始めた
「私ね、戦時中看護婦をやっていたの。何人もの焼かれ
た兵隊さんが運ばれてきてね……。
その匂いが忘れられないの……焼き魚の匂いなのよ
……」

「今の看護婦さんたちは優雅よね。あの時は人手不足で、寝ずに仕事をしたものよ」

そうか、それで焼き魚が食べられなくなったんだ……

苦しかった そんな思いも知りえないで

旦那様は先に他界してしまい 今では一人暮らしだそう

だ

「戦争はね、本当にあっちゃいけないのよ」

私はおばぁちゃんが焼き魚を食べたように箸で突っつく

のを見ながら

なんだか想像していた

シェルターにどんどん運ばれて来る怪我をした兵隊さん

対応に追われる看護婦さん

中には命が既に散った者たち

おばぁちゃんはきっと祈りきれない程祈ってきたのだろ

う

終戦を……

「桜が咲く頃退院でしょう？ウチに遊びにいらっしゃい

よ。田舎だけど、つくしが生えるから、一緒に摘み

ましょう。」

おばぁちゃんは嬉しそうに言った

「はい！」私も嬉しかった

実の祖母を亡くしてどのくらい経つだろう？

私のおばぁちゃんも戦時中父を連れて疎開した

シベリアで捕虜にされたおじぃちゃんを待ちながら……

桜の季節 約束通り看護婦のおばぁちゃんに逢いに行っ

た

駅からのバスからは桜並木が続いていて

最高のお天気だった

亡くなったおじぃちゃんの仏壇に手を合わせて

一緒につくしも摘んだ

たくさんおしゃべりをしてイチゴも食べた

帰り際、つくしのつくだ煮を持たせてくれた

手を振って

「またいらっしゃいね！」と笑っていた

――おばぁちゃん、ありがとう――

――焼き魚が食べられなくて当然だよ――

――元気でね！ また来るから――

戦争を知らない私に内緒で教えてくれたこと

胸が痛かったけれど、嬉しかったよ

桜は夕方の風に吹かれて舞い散っていた……

黒い傘

朝は晴天だった

明るい笑い声の中

私は心地良かった

私もいつかあの空のようになれるかな

もっともっと透明になれるかな

そんな思いが行く先を明るくした

もうじき　何かが起こる

はっきりとはわからないけれど

目には見えないけれど

もうじき　何かが起こる

昼は曇りだった

お弁当の白いお米まで

ねずみ色

朝の空に戻るかな

またキレイになれるかな

そんな思いで自分をだましていた

もうじき　何かが起こる
私には　まだわからないけれど
肌は何も感じないけれど
もうじき　何かが起こる

帰りは雨だった
私の青い傘は
元気に水をはじいてくれた
雨がやんだらまた晴天かな
今までで一番ステキな空になるかな
そんな思いはまだ消えなかった

もうじき　何かが起こる
誰にもわからないけれど
体温計も反応しないけれど
もうじき　何かが起こる

空を見上げた時
傘は黒かった
頬をつたう雨の粒が
世の中の汚れを詰め込んで
静かにこぼれおちていった

秋の空の下で

少し冷たくなった風に当たりながら
カフェテラスでサンドイッチをほおばって
イヤホンから流れる音楽に身を任せて
街行く人を眺めている

この日　この国では連休の始まり
行き交う人の　それぞれの忙しない感じや
休日を楽しむ様子
杖をついて歩く老人を見て
この国の今を少し感じた

車もバスも流れて
中には楽しそうに笑う子供もいて
自転車の親子連れも
犬を散歩する人も
そうだね「平和ボケ」と呼ばれたこの国の一角に自分も
いて……

此処で突然銃撃戦が起きたらどうなるか
此処で何も知らされないままに爆弾が落ちて命落とした

ら

この国の「平和」は一気に壊れる
砕け落ちる十代の夢のように……

私はこの国がキライじゃないんだ
むしろ好きになった
一度大嫌いになって飛び出してから
私の祖国は此処だと思い知った
だから守りたいんだ

何が出来るか
何処へ行けばいいのか
わからないけれど
愛している人の命がある事を
心から嬉しく思って
側にいられる事を感謝したいんだ

わからないなりに
私は書いて行くだろう

私は死ぬわけにはいかない

そう思って
ベビーカーを押すお父さんを見る

「平和ボケ」なんて言わせない
「平和」に
心から「平穏に」生きている人もいるのだ
だから許さない
たとえ許しても消える事のない傷跡を
この国にもたらす何かがあったら
私は生きて
生きて書き続けてやる

25

夢へと誘う旋律

その旋律はまるで子守唄のようにはじまる
マスターは大きく息を吸い少し間をおいて音を出す
静かにしずかに低い音から

子供たちはベッドにもぐり込み
その布団の中で肌の上をすべる心地よさに笑みを浮かべ
大人は目を閉じゆっくりと子供の頃を想い出す

マスターはつま先でリズムをとり
私たちをファンタジーの世界へと誘う

子供は橋を渡り川で魚釣りをし
おとなは大草原で風を感じる

ルーマニアの民族舞曲が奏でられたときには
子供は夢中でドラゴンと戦い
大人は夢の相手とダンスをする

マスターが全身でリズムをとり

その高音の震えが伝わる

子供はドラゴンを倒し王国を救い
大人は目をあけリンゴを摘む

激しく曲調が変わり
マスターは強く弦を奏でる
ホールが一体化しクライマックスを迎える
大かっさいがおこりマスターは満足気に深く頭を下げる
大きな花束を受け取りまたおじぎをする

こうして旋律は私たちの記憶にとどまり
おのおの夢を抱え外の風に当たりたくなる

26

癒しの土地

多国籍な土地の海沿いに並ぶカフェレストラン
軽い食事をしながら　いろいろな言語が飛び交い
小さい黒い鳥のように
少し遠くで波に乗るサーファー達
空も青く　白い鳥も飛んで
ヴァカンスを楽しむ　いつの時代もそこは
人を集め　最高の風景で皆を魅了し
昼間の暑い恋のように　毎日変わることなく
人々を少し酔わせる

陽が傾いてくると　あちこちでロウソクが灯され
海に沈んで行く太陽を見ようとまた人が集まる
ヤシの木が影を作り　その葉の間から
沈む太陽に照らされた海が静かに輝き
また今夜も変わらず　秘密を明かした後のように
人々を少し酔わせる

夜　空には少し欠けた月が昇る
海にも月は顔を重ね　また人を集める
今度は恋人達が　口づけを交わす場所となり

街は何も言わずに　その光景をポストカードにする
海は波の音だけで　恋人達を魅了して
ゆったりと　恐怖にも似た黒へと変わり
また人々を少し酔わせる

深夜　人々の気配はなく
あるのは　羽を伸ばした空と海
互いが互いを労り　愛の言葉をかけ合い
静かに静かに　この星を撫でるかのように包みこんで
またいつもそうだったように
生まれた姿で　この宇宙に青を発する

早朝を迎え　鳥たちが鳴くと
ジョギングをする人々が現れ
浮浪者も朝食の調達へ
少しすると　カフェも看板を出しまた人を集める
エスプレッソの香りと共に　寝ぼけ眼の旅人が
地図を広げてゆったりと海を眺めながら朝食をとる
ここは　人々の心の傷を隠す
ずっと昔からある癒しの土地
街がざわつき　空と海の恵みを受けながら
また新たな一日を始める

「Never End」
～交わされた約束とは?～

あの時　どんな約束が交わされたのだろう？
日本中が小室哲哉の楽曲で染まり
アムラーという現象が起きる程の
安室奈美恵の人気……

私は病を抱え留学先のアメリカから帰国
病を抱えてから　初めて母と訪れた沖縄
シーズンオフの四月
空も海も本土より青いと感じた

あの　カリフォルニアにいた時のように……
希望を持ってハンドルを握っていた
少し回復した時の私は
サミット前のホテルまで　車を飛ばした

大きな柱が並ぶホテルで
母と大きなソファに座り
アイスカフェ・オ・レを飲む
店員はフランスから来た留学生

会話も弾み　ゆったりと時間は流れた

どこかで　此処に「あの人」が来るんだと思いながら
「Never End」の意味を
その時代を生きる自分を
客観視しながら
本当に「Never End」でいいのか？と

沖縄出身の安室奈美恵がサミットで歌った曲
「Never End」に
「Never End　私たちの未来は／Never End　私たちの明
日は」
「数えきれない優しさが支えてる」
「忘れられない思い出の風が吹く」とある

伝わったのだろうか？
「Never End」は両国の関係ではなく
沖縄で起きた事実の傷跡ではないのか？
ことを荒だてたくない日本人の美徳と
少し臆病な精神を
わかったのだろうか？
「あの人たち」は

スモールワールド

ねぇ、世界は小さいって言うけれど本当かもね
願えば叶うって言うけれど本当かもね
世界は繋がっていて
みんなの願いが叶っていくのかもね

誰かが誰かの願いを叶えていて
祈りを悲しみを喜びを共にしていて
グローバリゼーションっていうけれど
その言葉の意味より奥深く心で
シンクロしているのかもね

だから悲しみが大きいとどんどん広がってしまうよ
涙の海が出来てしまう前に
止めないとね

絶対にダメだよって　これ以上の犠牲は哀しいよって
祈ることをしないとね　心からさ

ハヤという花

その花は棘を持たず
風にそよぐように飛んできた
産まれた土地を想い続け
自分の宿命を受け入れながらも

無残に踏まれて傷付いた小さな花たちのことを祈り続け
た

強風で折られた花や
花びら一枚一枚を祖国へと送り始めた
大きな花びらを増やし
自らの花びらを増やし
祖国に残された小さな「希望の花」たちのため
異国の地で懸命に咲きながら

茎の折れた花には茎を
花びらをちぎられた花には花びらを

無残に傷付けられた花たちの為に
また「再生」出来るように
ありったけの力で花を咲かせた

少しずつ周りの花たちも
「私にも何か出来ますか?」と
それぞれの花びらや茎を提供した

その時ハヤという名の花は大きく開花した

ハヤという花を知った他の花たちは
涙し 共感し
一輪の花では出来なかったことを
見事にやりのけた

国境をこえて
無くした茎や花びらの為に
風を使って
飛ばしたのだ

「愛」という自分の中に溢れる想い

祖国では
またあちこちで「希望の花」が咲き始め
ハヤに向かって綺麗な色とりどりの
お花畑を作っていった

ハヤという花は双方の国に名を残すだろう
しかし それがハヤの希望ではなかった

ハヤは祈った
「この世界で起きている事を知ってほしい」
「希望の花たちを、これ以上傷付けないで」
と

ハヤの祈りは大きく広がり
その種を世界中に
風に乗せて飛ばすであろう

この世界で
小さな「希望の花」が傷付けられなくなるまで
ハヤの祈りは続き
その花は大きく大きく咲き誇るだろう

Ⅲ章　ひだまり

一人の夕べ

静まる夜の空気の前の燃えたぎる太陽
背中に感じて一人苦しみに似た感情を抱く
何故人は人を
家族を他人を
愛し愛されたいのか?

自分の存在価値を確かめるようにセミの猛烈な鳴き声を
頭の中で響かせては虚しくなる今日の夕暮れ
昨日までの人
今日また会う人
すれ違うだけの人とも愛し合いたいのか?

ずっと待っていたこの時を
闇に消えゆく全ての者達が
眠り支度をする時覚醒する自分が切ない
何故人は人を
家族を他人を
愛し愛されたいのか?

まるで何も知らなかった赤子の時のように
母の胸の中で眠りたい…
そうだそんな幻想を抱いては拒絶が恐ろしい
何故人は人を
家族を他人を
愛し愛されたいのか?

自己暗示にかけて安らいでいる不幸だと思わせる錯覚が
今夜もやって来る
この痛みを
この妄想を
私は愛さなければならないのか?

未だわからぬままに
夕暮れは訪れ
かすかに聞こえるセミの声と共に
この夏を感じている

心のレース

私の心はママが編んでくれた
白いレース

fragile だけど柔らかいレース

一針一針ていねいに編んでくれた

でも、いつからかな？
小さな穴があいたと思ったら
ホロホロほどけてしまって
いつの間にか大きな穴になっていた

ママは慌てて
そのレースに手を入れたけれど
前のようにはゆかない

私がママ以外の人に心を明け渡したせいだ
ママ、ごめんなさい
私、なんとか自分でまた編むよ

きっときっと前とは違うかもしれないけれど
きれいなレースに仕上げるよ

ママ、泣かないで
ママ、心配しないで

今流行りのものには出来ないかもしれないけれど…

私の心は
ママが編んでくれた白いレース

fragile だけど
柔らかいレース

ほどけた糸をゆっくりと指に巻いて
胸にあてた

峠

父は峠を越えた

今朝
足の爪のマニキュアが剝げているのが歪んで見えた
透明で滑らかで それでいてどこか重い……
バスタブのお湯が静かに揺れている

その時父は「心が解放されるんだ」と言った
父と一緒に病室でイヤホン片方ずつ聴いたのを思っていた
部屋では「アルハンブラの思い出」がかかっていて

静かに祈るしかなかった
また父が自分の好きな詩やエッセイを書けるよう

目と目を合わせて会話が出来たことを　皆に感謝した
また果てしない旅へと逝く前に
父に会いに来て
しかし今回
いつも周りはうるさい

夕食はコンビニのゆで卵二つ
表に出る気にはなれなかった
少し開いた窓から
クルマが雨を潰す音がする

明日になればまた違う日
父の苦しそうな呼吸が私の耳で鳴っていて
そのまま薬を飲んで眠ろうとする
夢を見ているようだ
異空間の中　何処か遠い旅に出た気になった

33

鼓動

オイルの香りがするジッポ
いつも平穏な心を保つ為に
父は銀製品を静かに磨いていた

幼い頃よくお風呂に入れてくれたそうだ
大きくなると
お風呂場からは
シャンソンを歌う父

女の子なのに
グローブを付けてキャッチボール
公園で何度も転びながら
自転車の乗り方を教わり
川辺の道を一緒にサイクリング
夏休みには八ヶ岳へ
山登りは大の苦手で困らせた

離れて暮らすようになって
喧嘩も増えて

父を恨んだ時期があった
父は持病に悩まされる
酸素ボンベのことを
「宇宙遊泳」だと書いていた

狂ったように泣いた日

父は必死に生きた

ドクンドクンドクン……

ずっと側に感じている
導いてくれている
書くことをやめない私がいる

シュッと磨かれたジッポ
揺らめく火
夜の中で

ドクン……

父に包まれて

鳥のさえずりの前に目が覚めた
少し肌寒くて静かな朝……

ここへ来られた
父がずっと待っていたかのように
穏やかで　落ち着いた気持ち

膨大な量の蔵書を
思い出の品を
どうするか？

今はただ
父との時間を大切にしたい
インスタントコーヒーを飲みながら
少しずつ明るくなる外の光を感じている

父はいる
ここにもいる
私の中にもいる

そして　父を忘れない人びとの中にも

鳥の鳴き声
父の鼓動を感じる
ここに後悔だらけの
情けない私がいて
父は温かく見守る

今　父は見ている
私の全てを
地からも
天からも
―ずっと見守っているよ―

こうして生まれる連鎖が
どこかで人に理性をもたらすのだろうか？
―悪い事なんてできないね―
心ではにかんだ

赤いスポーツカーの模型
私がニューヨークで買ってあげたんだ

35

ちゃんと飾っててくれたんだね
ついでに私の写真も

薄明かりの表では
鳥たちがますます鳴き出して
一日を始めようとしている

赤松の
ひっそり佇む
息吹かけ
大黒柱
亡きあとにも

父の家はまるで主人を喪ったようではなく
むしろ生かしている
そんなふうに感じて

父との思い出がまた増えた気がした

アロマ

母のお見舞いに行った夜
夜中まで眠れなくて
ソファの前のテーブルに飾ってある
父とのツーショットの写真を眺めながら
ピアノ音楽を聴いてみる

——居ないなんて信じられないんだ——
ちょっと旅行に行っているだけ

父の顔がやわらいで
温かな眼差しで私を見ているかのよう
そんな気になった……

猫たちも眠れずにボールで遊んでいる
イヤフォンから流れてくる
ピアノ音楽は心にも心地よく
父と一緒に何度も観た「紅の豚」を思い返している

母はそろそろ起きる時間

体温を計り
夜中のトイレの回数を聞かれ
寝ぼけまなこでなんとか立ち上がるのだろう
―パパ、ママ転んじゃったよ―
―酷い痛みなの。　側にいてあげてね―

アロマが香る
ピアノ音楽にのせて
外が暗闇から薄明るくなる頃

病院で一人

夕暮れ時の病院のベンチで
一人緑を眺め
鳥の鳴き声を聞いている母

きっとその病院でも母は外国人一人
皆に良くしてもらっているとはいえ
私の中でいつも何処かで孤独を感じている母がいる

母を一人にはしないのに
私にそのキャパシティがあれば……
毎日お見舞いに行けたら

母は笑って話す
売店で買ったチョコレートの話や
マイカーを持つ看護婦さんの話

「立派だよ
自然の力を借りながら
ママは自分の道を歩んでるよ」

37

緑が
鳥のさえずりが
母を癒し助ける

後もう少し
自分の家に帰るまで

二足歩行の未熟者

空洞が出来た心に風が通り
ヒリヒリと痛みを増している
傷口を大きく開かれたようになって
手当の術がわからない……

父の肩に乗っかり
ケラケラと笑ったのは
母の腕に抱かれ
スヤスヤと眠ったのは
幾億年前だろう……

私はあれから三十以上は歳を取った
そしてその記憶は億へと昔に追いやられた
父のゴツゴツした手が懐かしい
母の柔らかい胸が恋しい
いつから二足歩行の未熟者として歩いて来たのか……

手当の出来ない傷を負い
それでもまた人を愛し

愛されたいと願い
行く末は愛を愛猫に向けるしか出来ず
独りよがりな生活を続けている

声が聞きたい
触れたい
抱きしめられたい
「愛しているよ」と
強く強くどこまでも持っていかれるように
さらってほしい
そして連れ戻してほしい
幾億年前の暖かな日差しの
あの家と父と母の息づかいを感じる場所へと

二足歩行の未熟者は不器用だから
何度転んでも同じ石でつまずいてしまう
心に出来た空洞もそのままで
それでもいつか
幾億年前のあなた方が蘇る時
私は本当の意味でこの二本足で立てるのかもしれない

……

野生の記憶

猫が風を見つめる時
遠い先祖の足跡が
砂に舞って消える

枯れた木の枝に
散らかした肉の残骸を残して
夢をみる

太陽が傾いて
猫も目を細めている時
ジッと過去が私を見ている

野生の一部が
心の安定を促して
無駄のない体で横たえる姿が
未知の世界を近くに感じさせる

過去に残した足跡
舞ってしまった何か

未来に向けて見据える今
静かな一歩を踏み出す

何処かで誰かと

私の親指を甘噛みする牙はまだ小さいけれど鋭く
その力で私に痛みを与えないように
戯れて甘えて舌で舐める優しさ

まだ一月で母親から離れたこの仔達が私に与える安らぎ
と
まだ母親になりきれない自分の小さな苛立ちに
彼女達は気付いているのだろうか？

時々煙たそうに見るその目や
黄昏たような顔
きょとんとした表情も
全て本当はこの仔達の母親が見ていたであろう姿

私が今　この仔達と出逢い
ノラとしてではなく
家族として家に迎え入れ
どこか不安を抱えたまま　なんとか愛を
与え与えられている

何処かの国で銃を手にした子供がいて
それらを教えた大人がいて
家族は皆いるはずなのに
見られない笑顔や至福の瞬間

今まさにこの時
何処かで母親から引き離された子供がいて
泣いている母親もいる
そして私の膝の上で子猫がニャッと鳴き
ジッと私を見るのである

何処かで　何処かで
いつか　いつか
誰かと誰かが
争いではない繋がりを
求め与えられ
どんな形でもいいから
家族となって　この星で
胸を癒してほしい……

ひだまり

初春の午後のベッドの上に
ほんわりとひだまりができて
指をスルスルと猫の毛の間に潜ませて
目を閉じて感じる鼓動

抱っこは嫌がるのに
こうして共にベッドに潜り込むのは
すっかりなじみになっていて
痛みを感じ取ってくれているかのように
そっと寄り添ってくれる

窓から射す光が
私たちを照らして
この家の中で静かな幸福（しあわせ）を作る
ひだまりに包まれて愛を感じている
あの日のように……

滑らせる手を猫は心地よく受け止めて
私は精一杯の愛で撫でてやる

あなたが私にそうしたように
安心感という愛撫をこの仔たちに与えたい
レースのカーテンが少し揺れて
私たちはそれぞれの夢を見る

一時だったとしても
こうしている瞬間がこの上ない幸せで
この季節を　この鼓動を
ゆっくり心に刻む
愛を感じるってこういうのかな？
なんて思いながら……

想いは巡り
私の腕枕で眠る猫達が少しの寝息をたてている時
どこまでも果てしない心地よさの中に
消えていくひだまりが
ぽっかりと寂しさを呼ぶ

ほんの一瞬　暖められた部屋で
私は猫達と夢を見た
あの時のあのままのあなたの後ろ姿

遠くに見えて消えて行って目が覚めた
手はギュッと猫の背中を掴んでいた

枕に顔を埋めて　少し生温かい涙を
声をこらえるようにして流してから
布団の中から私を見る猫達に微笑んで
私は立ち上がる
そんな繰り返しの中でも
この仔達が来てから涙の数は減ったんだ

―何があっても前向きに―
そう決めた今年の抱負
頭のどこかに置いて
コーヒーを入れにキッチンへと向かう
消えたひだまりのぬくもりと猫達をベッドに残して……

解説「世界はつながっている」という強い思い

鈴木比佐雄

井上摩耶英日詩集
『SMALL WORLD／スモールワールド』に寄せて

井上摩耶氏はすでに四冊の詩集と一冊の詩画集を刊行している詩人で、第四詩集で第50回横浜詩人会賞を受賞し、その詩篇は詩の批評家たちからも高く評価されている。今回この五冊から選ばれた三十四篇とそれを英訳した詩が合体された英日詩集が刊行された。井上氏は略歴で「シリア系フランス人の母と日本人の父の間で横浜に生まれる」と記している。母はフランス語が母国語で英語も堪能であり、亡くなった父は仏文学者で詩人の井上輝夫だったので、父母とは日本語だけでなくフランス語や英語でも会話しあっているのだろう。つまり井上氏と父母は三ヵ国語を話すトリリンガルな関係だったのだろう。ただ井上氏の母国語は日本語であり、英詩としての完璧を期すために詩人で英語学者の与那覇恵子氏に翻訳を依頼した。井上氏は母やフランス・アメリカなどに暮らす親族や留学時代の友人たちにも自分の詩を読んでもらいたいという思いがあった。と同時に自分の関係す

る「スモールワールド」を世界の多くの人びとに読んでもらいたいと願ったのだろう。本詩集はⅠ章「通り雨」、Ⅱ章「スモールワールド」、Ⅲ章「ひだまり」に分けられている。Ⅰ章の冒頭の詩「通り雨」の初めの三連を引用したい。

土のにおいが舞い上がる／初夏の通り雨／屋根のあるところから／そっと感じている／／緑がよろこぶだろうな／花が野が／田んぼが畑が／よろこぶだろうな／／人は傘や種を探すけれど／自然には不可欠な雨／なんだか不思議／共存していることが

Standing under the roof ／ during a passing shower
in early summer ／ I smell the dust
／ thrown up by the rain. ／／ Greens may be
happy now. ／ Flowers and plants,
vegetable fields— ／ all may be happy now. ／／ People
are busy looking for roofs and umbrellas. ／ But rain
is necessary for Nature. ／ It is strange ／ that we are
living together

日本語で表現されている「通り雨」はとても繊細な感受性だ。一連目は初夏の晴れた青空の下で乾いた土の上に、雨雲が空を覆い雨が突然降ってくる。井上氏は屋根のある所に避難して、雨が上がるのを待っている。すると雨に打たれた土が舞い上がって井上氏は土のにおいを感じてしまう。この場面は浮世絵に描かれた「にわか雨」のようで、井上氏は歌川広重「東海道五十三次」の大磯での「通り雨」にタイムスリップしているかのように雨を詩にしている。また自然の変化を楽しむ日本人の暮らしの感受性を見事に表現している。このようなことを日本人の感受性と限定することは間違いであり、多様な国々でそのような自然の繊細な変化を楽しむ民衆は世界中に存在していると井上氏は暗示しているかのようだ。

二連目は自然の植物の気持ちを代弁するかのように、「緑がよろこぶだろうな」と語る。雨を避けようとする人間に対して、雨を歓喜している植物たちの気持ちに成り代わっている。同じ雨なのに人と植物の感じ方がこれほど異なることに気づき「なんだか不思議」と語っている。井上氏は人と植物の両方の気持ちを取り持つような、目に見えないけれどもこの生きている世界で「共存していること」の「不思議」さを感受してしまう詩人なのだ。

翻訳者の与那覇氏は井上氏のそんな感受性のリズムやイメージを日本語が隠している主語を補いながら英語のリズムに見事に英訳している。

地球環境が経済活動による人間の欲望で急速に破壊されつつある情況で、自然への敬意をいかに取り戻し、本来的で持続可能な人間の生き方が根源的な問題として問われている。その際に井上氏の「通り雨」のような感受性を取り戻すことが大切だと思われてならない。つまり「スモールワールド」の感受性が世界を変えていくことになるのだという思いが井上氏にあるだろう。最後に詩「スモールワールド」の冒頭の一連を引用して、この小論を終えたい。

「ねえ、世界は小さいって言うけれど本当かもね／願えば叶うって言うけれど本当かもね／世界が繋がっていて／みんなの願いが叶っていくのかもね」この「世界はつながっている」という強い思いが、英日詩集『SMALL WORLD／スモールワールド』を作り出した井上氏に存在するのであり、今後も詩を書き続ける詩的精神になっていくのだと私には思われてならない。そんな井上氏のみずみずしい三十四篇を英語と日本語で読んで欲しいと願っている。

あとがきに代えて

この度は、私の初の英日詩集を手に取って下さる皆様に感謝します。以前から、日本語以外の言語で詩集を出したいと思っていましたが、なかなか機会がありませんでした。今回は、コールサック社の鈴木比佐雄氏のお陰で詩人・評論家・英語教育者・同時通訳者である与那覇恵子氏に引き合わせて頂き、私の長年の夢が叶いました。

母や、その親族、友人は、私が日本語でしか詩を書かないので、「摩耶は一体何を書いているんだ?」といつも母に尋ねて来ていたそうです。この詩集のお陰で、そう言った身近な人たちに、私の作品を読んでもらえる事、大変嬉しく思います。この英日詩集の実現のために編集をし解説文も執筆された鈴木氏や、私の詩を見事に翻訳して下さった与那覇氏に心より感謝しています。

表紙の写真は、若かりし母と、まだ幼い私でした。そして、今は亡き父であるが、この写真を撮ったのは父でした。写真には写ってないが、ここに三人がいます。私

の原点でありこの三人で作り上げた小さな家族の「スモールワールド」が存在しました。

そこから、世界に向けて来た目や感覚、父や母から教わった沢山の事柄、今、この時代はまさに世界が「スモールワールド」になっていると思います。いつの間にか、現代という「スモールワールド」の内から外からその言葉の意味の深さや、豊かさを得たり、時に少し窮屈さなどを感じながら生きています。

世界中の人が、頭や心の中で平和をイメージし、それぞれの幸せを願えば、この広い世界も幸多い「スモールワールド」になるし、争いや、お互いの粗探しをしていたら、それはそれで窮屈な「スモールワールド」になります。インターネットや、無料通話のお陰で、どれだけ便利になったか。その豊かさに感謝しつつも、まだまだ続いているこの世界の悲劇で傷ついた多くの人びとの為に祈りたい。

この詩集の中にある、「ハヤという花」という詩は、私のハトコで、シリアからアメリカに移住したハヤという娘に捧げる詩となっています。ハヤは、ずっとガールスカウトに参加しながら、アメリカに移住して、UCLA(カリフォルニア大学ロサンゼルス校)に入ったとき

46

には、教会を通して、シリアの紛争で足や手を無くした子供達や犠牲者に義足や義手を提供するNPO法人を立ち上げました。各メディアに取り上げられ、その働きかけは大きく広がっています。そんなハヤの想いに感動し、その祈りや心を繋ぎたいと、ハヤに捧げる詩を書きました。この詩が、更に多くの人々の心に触れることが出来れば幸いです。

この英日詩集が、貴方にとってどんな書物になるのか、私にはわからない。しかし、共に共有し、共にこの時代に生き、日本語だけではなく、もう少し広い視野で私の詩をより多くの人が読んでもらえたなら、私は素直に嬉しく、貴方の心の中に少しでも何かを残せれば、それはまたとても嬉しいことなのです。

この度は本当にありがとうございました！

2019年12月吉日

井上摩耶

著者略歴

井上　摩耶（いのうえまや）

一九七六年、シリア系フランス人の母と日本人の父の間に横浜で生まれる。日本、フランス、アメリカで生活経験。アイデンティティに悩みながら、舞台美術などを学ぶ。インターネット上や文芸誌「コールサック」に詩を発表。父親である故・井上輝夫（一九四〇～二〇一五、詩人・フランス文学者）著『聖シメオンの木菟　シリア・レバノン紀行』（ミッドナイト・プレス）の再版を刊行。

既刊著書

・詩集『Look at me ―たとえばな詩―』
（ミッドナイト・プレス）

・詩集『レイルーナ ―はかない愛のたとえばな詩―』
（ミッドナイト・プレス）

・詩集『闇の炎』（コールサック社）

・井上摩耶×神月ROI　詩画集
『Particulier ～国境の先へ～』（コールサック社）

・詩集『鼓動』（コールサック社）

・英日詩集『SMALL WORLD　スモールワールド』
（コールサック社）

現住所

〒二二七―〇〇四三

横浜市青葉区藤が丘二―三七―二　グリーンヒルb三〇二

48